The Cherry Orchard

WORKS BY DAVID MAMET
Published by Grove Press

PLAYS

American Buffalo
Glengarry Glen Ross
Goldberg Street: Short Plays and Monologues
A Life in the Theatre
Reunion and *Dark Pony*
Sexual Perversity in Chicago and *The Duck Variations*
Speed-the-Plow
The Shawl and *Prairie du Chien*
Three Children's Plays:
    The Poet and the Rent
    The Frog Prince
    *The Revenge of the Space Pandas or Binky Rudich and the
        Two-Speed Clock*
The Woods, Lakeboat, Edmond

SCREENPLAYS

Five Television Plays:
    A Waitress in Yellowstone
    Brandford
    The Museum of Science and Industry Story
    A Wasted Weekend
    We Will Take You There
Homicide
House of Games
Things Change
We're No Angels

ADAPTATIONS BY DAVID MAMET

The Cherry Orchard, by Anton Chekhov
The Three Sisters, by Anton Chekhov
Uncle Vanya, by Anton Chekhov

The Cherry Orchard
BY ANTON CHEKHOV

ADAPTED BY DAVID MAMET FROM
A LITERAL TRANSLATION BY PETER NELLES

**GROVE PRESS
NEW YORK**

Published simultaneously in Canada
Printed in the United States of America

Library of Congress Cataloging-in-Publication Data

Mamet, David.
The cherry orchard.
I. Chekhov, Anton Pavlovich, 1860–1904. Vishnevyîsad.
II. Title.
PS3563.A4345C5   1986   812'.54   86-45246
ISBN 0-8021-3002-X (pbk.)

Grove Press
841 Broadway
New York, NY 10003

00 01 02   15 14 13 12 11 10 9 8

Notes on *The Cherry Orchard*

When playing poker it is a good idea to determine what cards your opponents might be playing. There are two ways to do this. One involves watching their idiosyncrasies—the way they hold their cards when bluffing as opposed to the way they hold them when they have a strong hand; their unconscious self-revelatory gestures; the way they play with their chips when unsure. This method of gathering information is called looking for "tells."

The other way to gather information is to analyze your opponent's hand according to what he *bets*.

These two methods are analogous—in the theatre—to a concern with *characterization*, and a concern with *action;* or, to put it a bit differently: a concern with the *way* a character does something and, on the other hand, the actual *thing that he does*.

I recently worked on an adaptation of *The Cherry Orchard*.

My new-found intimacy with the play led me to look past the quiddities of the characters and examine what it is that they are actually doing. I saw this:

The title is a flag of convenience. Nobody in the play gives a damn about the cherry orchard.

In the first act Lyubov returns. We are informed

that her beloved Estate is going to be sold unless someone acts quickly to avert this catastrophe.

She is told this by the rich Lopakhin. He then immediately tells her that he has a plan: cut down the cherry orchard, raze the house and build tract housing for the summer people.

This solution would save (although alter) the estate.

Lopakhin keeps reiterating his offer throughout the play. Lyubov will not accept. Lopakhin finally buys the estate.

"Well," one might say, "one cannot save one's beloved cherry orchard by cutting it down." That, of course, is true. But, in the text, other alternatives are offered.

Reference is made to the Rich Aunt in Yaroslavl ("Who is so very rich"), and who adores Lyubov's daughter, Anya. A flying mendicant mission is proposed but never materializes. The point here is not that this mission is viewed as a good bet, it isn't, but that, if the action of the protagonist (supposedly Lyubov) were to save the cherry orchard, she would grasp *any* possibility of help.

The more likely hope of salvation is fortuitous marriage. Gaev, Lyubov's brother, in enumerating the alternatives lists: inheriting money, begging from the rich aunt, marrying Anya off to a rich man.

The first is idle wishing, and we've struck off the second, but what about the third alternative?

There's nobody much around for Anya. But what about her stepsister, Varya?

Varya, Lyubov's adopted daughter, is not only nubile, she is *in love*. With whom is she in love? She is in love with Lopakhin.

Why, *Hell*. If I wanted to save *my* cherry orchard, and *my* adopted daughter was in love (and we are told that her affections are by no means abhorrent to their recipient) with the richest man in town, what would *I* do? What would *you* do? It's the easy way out, the play ends in a half-hour and everybody gets to go home early.

But Lyubov does *not* press this point, though she makes reference to it in every act. She does *not* press on to a happy marriage between Varya and Lopakhin. Nor, curiously, is this match ever mentioned as a solution for the problem of the cherry orchard. The problem of the botched courtship of Varya and Lopakhin exists only as one of a number of supposed sub-plots. (More on this later.)

In the penultimate scene of the play Lyubov, who is leaving the now-sold estate to return to Paris, attempts to tie up lose ends. She exhorts Lopakhin to propose to Varya, and he says he will. Left alone, Lopakhin loses his nerve and does not propose. Why does Lyubov, on learning this, not press her case? Why did she not do so sooner?

Even now, at the end of the play, if Lyubov *really* cared about the cherry orchard, she could save it from the ax. She could easily *force* Lopakhin to propose to Varya, and then get the bright idea that all of them could live on the estate as one happy family. And Lopakhin would not refuse her.

But she does not do so. Is this from lack of inventiveness? No. It is from lack of concern. The cherry orchard is not her concern.

What about Lopakhin? Why is *he* cutting down the cherry orchard? He has been, from youth, infatuated with Lyubov. She is a goddess to him, her estate is a fairyland to him, and his great desire in the play is to please her. (In fact, if one were to lapse into a psychological overview of the play at this point one might say that the reason Lopakhin can't propose to Varya is that he is in love with Lyubov.)

Lopakhin buys the estate. For ninety-thousand rubles, which means nothing to him. He then proceeds to cut down the trees, which he knows will upset his goddess, Lyubov; and to raze the manor house. His parents were slaves in that house, Lyubov grew up in the house, he doesn't need the money, why is he cutting down the trees? (Yes, yes, yes; we encounter halfhearted addenda in re: future generations being won back to the land. But it doesn't wash. Why? If Lopakhin wanted to build a summer colony he could build it anywhere. He could have built it without Lyubov's land, and without her permission. If his objective were the building of summer homes and he were faced with two tracts, one where he had to cut down his idol's home, and one where he did not, which would he pick? Well, he has an infinite number of tracts. He can build anywhere he wants. Why cut down the trees and sadden his beloved idol? Having bought the estate he could easily let it sit, and, should the spirit move him subsequently, build his resort elsewhere.)

What, in effect, is going on here?

Nothing that has to do with trees.

The play is a series of scenes about sexuality, and, particularly, frustrated sexuality.

The play was inspired, most probably, by the scene in *Anna Karenina* between Kitty's friend, Mlle. Varenka, and her gentleman companion, Mr. Koznyshez.

The two of them, lonely, nice people, are brought together through the office of mutual friends. Each should marry, they are a perfect match. In one of the finest scenes in the book we are told that each knew the time had arrived, that it was Now or Never. They go for a walk, Mr. Koznyshez is about to propose when a question about mushrooms comes to his mind, the mood is broken, and so the two nice people are doomed to loneliness.

If this description sounds familiar it should. Chekhov, pregnant of his theme, lifted it shamelessly (and probably unconsciously) from Tolstoy and gave it to Lopakhin and Varya.

Not only do *they* play out the scene, EVERYBODY IN THE PLAY PLAYS OUT THE SAME SCENE.

Anya is in love with Petya Trofimov, the tutor of her late brother. Trofimov is in love with *her*, but is too repressed to make the first move. He, in fact, declares that he is above love, while, in a soliloquy, refers to Anya as "My springtime, my dear morning sun."

Yepihkodov, the estate bookkeeper, is in love with Dunyasha, the chambermaid. He keeps trying to propose, but she thinks him a boor and will not hear him out. *She* is in love with Yasha, Lyubov's footman. Yasha seduces and abandons her as he is in love with himself.

Lyubov herself is in love. She gave her fortune to her paramour and nursed him through three years of his sickness. He deserted her for a younger woman.

Now: *this* is the reason she has returned to the estate. It is purely coincidental that she returns just prior to the auction of the orchard. *Why* is it coincidental? Because, as we have seen, she doesn't come back to *save* it. If she wanted to she could. *Why* does she come back? What is the event which prompts her return? Her jilting. What is the event that prompts her to return again to Paris? The continual telegrams of her roué lover begging for forgiveness.

Why did Lyubov come home? To lick her wounds, to play for time, to figure out a new course for her life.

Now: none of these is a theatrically compelling action. (The last comes closest, but it could be done in seclusion and does not need other characters. As, indeed, *Lyubov* is, essentially a monologue—there's nothing she *wants* from anyone on stage.)

If Lyubov is doing nothing but these solitary, reflective acts, why is she the protagonist of the play? She *isn't*.

The play has no protagonist. It has a couple of squad leaders. The reason it has no protagonist is that it has no through-action. It has one scene repeated by various couples.

To continue: Lyubov's brother is Gaev. He is a perennial bachelor, and is referred to several times in the text as an old lady. What does *he* want? Not much of anything. Yes, he cries at the end when the orchard is cut down. But he appears to be just as happy going to work in the bank and playing caroms as he is lounging around the morning room and playing caroms.

The other odd characters are Firs, the ancient butler, who is happy the mistress has returned, and Semeonov Pischick, a poor neighbor, who is always looking on the bright side.

He, Firs, and Gaev are local color. They are all celibate, and seen as somewhat doddering in different degrees. And they are all happy. Because they are not troubled by Sex. They are not involved in the play's one and oft-repeated action: to consummate, clarify, or rectify an unhappy sexual situation.

The cherry orchard and its imminent destruction is nothing other than an effective dramatic device.

The play is not "If you don't pay the mortgage I'll take your cow." It is "Kiss me quick because I'm dying of cancer."

The *obstacle* in the play does not grow out of, and does not even *refer* to the actions of the characters. The play works because it is a compilation of brilliant scenes.

I would guess—judging from its similarity to many of his short stories—that he wrote the scenes between the servant girl Dunyasha and Yepikhodov first. That perhaps sparked the idea of a scene between Dunyasha and the man *she* loves, Yasha, a footman just returned from Paris. Who did this fine footman return with? The mistress. *Et ensuite.*

To continue this conceit: what did Chekhov do when he had two hours worth of scenes and thirteen characters running around a country house? He had, as any playwright has, three choices.

He could shelve the material as brilliant sketches; he could *examine* the material and attempt to discern any intrinsically dramatic through-action, and extrapolate the play out of *that*. (Compare the structure of *The Cherry Orchard* with that of *The Seagull*. In *The Seagull* Arkadina wants to recapture her Youth, which causes her to devote herself to a younger man, and ignore the needs of her son whose age is an affront to her pretensions of youth. He struggles to obtain her respect and the respect and love of Nina, who (another actress) represents one split-off aspect of Arkadina's personality, i.e., her available sexuality. *The Seagull* is structured as a tragedy. At the end of the play the hero, Treplev, undergoes recognition of his state and reversal of his situation—he kills himself. What happens at the end of *The Cherry Orchard*? Everyone goes home—they go back to doing *exactly* what they were doing before the play began. You might say *The Cherry Orchard* is structured as a *farce*. That is the dramatic form to which it is closest. One might also say that it is close to a series of revue sketches with a common theme, and, in fact, it is. The play is most closely related to, and is probably the first example of the twentieth-century phenomenon of the revue-play . . . the *theme* play, e.g. *La Ronde, Truckline Cafe, Men in White, Waters of the Moon,* etc.)

To return: Chekhov has thirteen people stuck in a summer house. He has a lot of brilliant scenes. His third alternative is to come up with a pretext which will keep them in the same place and *talking* to each other for a while. This is one of the alternatives and dilemmas of the modern dramatist: "Gosh, this material is *fantastic*. What can I do to just keep the people in the house?"

One can have a piece of jewelry stolen, one can have a murder committed, one can have a snowstorm, one can have the car break down, one can have The Olde Estate due to be sold for debts in three weeks unless someone comes up with a good solution.

I picture Chekhov coming up with this pretext and saying, "Naaaa, they'll never go for it." I picture him watching rehearsals and *wincing* every time Lopakhin says (as he says frequently): "Just remember, you have only three (two, one) weeks until the cherry orchard is to be sold." "Fine," he must have thought. "That's real playwriting. One doesn't see Horatio coming out every five minutes and saying, 'Don't forget, Hamlet, your uncle killed your dad and now he's sleeping with your Ma!'"

"Oh no," he must have thought, "I'll never get away with it." But he did, and left us a play we cherish.

Why do we cherish the play? Because it is about the struggle between the Old Values of the Russian Aristocracy and their loosening grasp on power? I think not. For, finally, a play is about—and is *only* about—the actions of its characters. We, as audience, understand a play not in terms of the superficial idiosyncrasies or social *states* of its characters (they, finally, *separate* us from the play), but only in terms of the *action* the characters are trying to accomplish. (Set *Hamlet* in Waukegan and it's still a great play.)

The enduring draw of *The Cherry Orchard* is not that it is set in a dying Czarist Russia or that it has rich folks and poor folks. We are drawn to the play because it speaks to our *subconscious*—which is what a play should do. And we subconsciously perceive and enjoy the reiterated action of this reiterated scene: two people at odds—each trying to fulfill his or her frustrated sexuality.

David Mamet

The Cherry Orchard

David Mamet's adaptation of *The Cherry Orchard* was first presented at The Goodman Theatre of the Arts Institute of Chicago in a Chicago Theatre Groups, Inc. production in March 1985 with the following cast:

Lyubov Ranevskaya	*Lindsay Crouse*
Anya	*Nessa Rabin*
Varya	*Lisa Zane*
Leonid Gaev	*Colin Stinton*
Yermolay Lopakhin	*Peter Riegert*
Petya Trofimov	*W.H. Macy*
Semeonov-Pishchik	*Mike Nussbaum*
Charlotta	*Linda Kimbrough*
Yepikhodov	*Lionel Mark Smith*
Dunyasha	*Kathleen Dennehy*
Firs	*Les Podewell*
Yasha	*José Santana*
A Stranger	*Robert Scogin*
Station Master	*Robert Scogin*

Directed by GREGORY MOSHER

THE CHARACTERS

Lyubov Ranevskaya, a landowner	Charlotta, a governess
Anya, her daughter	Yepikhodov, a clerk
Varya, her adopted daughter	Dunyasha, a maid
Leonid Gaev, her brother	Firs, a valet
Yermolay Lopakhin, a merchant	Yasha, a young valet
Petya Trofimov, a student	A Stranger
Semeonov-Pishchik, a landowner	Station Master

THE SCENE: Ranevskaya's estate, 1904.

Act One

Lopakhin: I think the train woke me. (*Pause.*) What time is it?

Dunyasha: About two. (*Puts out candle.*) Huh. It's almost light.

Lopakhin: How late was the train?

Dunyasha: Two hours.

Lopakhin: Why didn't you wake me?

Dunyasha: I thought you'd left.

Lopakhin: . . . Come here to meet the train n'I oversleep. That's fine . . .

Dunyasha: Ah! That's . . . hear . . . hear it. . . ? They're . . . it's them.

Lopakhin: No please, they've got five years worth of baggage. It's going to take them awhile. (*Pause.*) Five years. Do you know—I remember her. I was fifteen. My father rest in peace, we were down at his store. And he hit me. He was drunk. She was there, Lyubov Andreevna. (*Pause.*) He hit me in the yard she—just a young girl then—she led me to the pump. She washed my face, for I was bleeding—washed my face and said "Don't cry. Don't cry, for time heals everything—don't cry my little peasant. Everything will be well by your wedding day." (*Pause.*) Well . . . my father was a peasant. Certainly. And I am, too. Yes. White vest, yellow shoes. Perfume on a pig. Well—I worked for it . . . you know why, though, I was reading the *book*, I fell asleep—I'll tell you why: I couldn't understand it. (*Pause.*)

Dunyasha: You couldn't understand. . . ?

Lopakhin: The book.

Dunyasha: Dogs didn't sleep.

Lopakhin: Mm?

Dunyasha: The dogs didn't sleep all night. They, you know, *sensed* the masters were coming home.

Lopakhin (*simultaneously with "home"*)**:** Excuse me, please, but Dunyasha, why does an educated girl like you . . .

Dunyasha: I'm shaking like a leaf. I'm going to faint.

Lopakhin (*simultaneously with "faint"*): No—you aren't going to faint—why should you faint? Why do you have to faint, fine as you are? *Dressed* like a lady, made up like a—

Yepikhodov (**Yepikhodov** *enters with flowers.*) (*To* **Dunyasha**): Th' gardener sent 'em. He says put 'em in the dining room.

Lopakhin: And could I have some kvass?

Dunyasha: Of course. (*Exits.*)

Yepikhodov: Frost.

Lopakhin: Mm. Ah.

Yepikhodov: Three degrees of frost.

Lopakhin: Is that so?

Yepikhodov: Frost and cherries in bloom. That's not right. And it's the climate. There is a time to *reap* and a time to *rest*—and *further—yesterday,* the day before yesterday I bought *boots.* And I *assure* you, what do they do? *Squeak.* And so what do you do for *that?*

Lopakhin: Mm. Hmm. *Look:*

Yepikhodov: *Every day.* Every day of my life—what do I do? *Complain?* No—*smile.* What is misfortune? Every misfortune is just a *test.*

7

Lopakhin: I'm sure it is. (*Takes kvass from* **Dun-yasha**.)

Yepikhodov (*simultaneously with "is" to* **Dunyasha**): Ah. Hello. I was just. . . (*Bumps into chair*.) You *see?* You *see?* And excuse me for *saying* so, but: Q.E.D. I rest my . . . (*Exits*.)

Pause.

Dunyasha: He proposed to me.

Lopakhin: Hmmm.

Dunyasha: Yes. (*Pause*.) Huh, um . . . He's a . . . you know . . . he's a, I suppose he's a nice enough man, but I don't understand a thing he . . . a nice enough man. *Good* . . . I suppose . . . *sensitive* . . . I (*pause*) I *like* him—but I don't understand him. And he worships me. And then he bumps into a chair. Do you know what we call him?

Lopakhin: No.

Dunyasha: "Endless Misfortune."

Lopakhin: Who calls him?

Dunyasha (*simultaneously with "him"*): The servants.

Lopakhin (*jumping up*): Ah. Ah. Yes! You hear them!!

Dunyasha: Oh, my God, I've turned cold. They're coming.

Lopakhin: That's them. That's them, *finally* . . . after, after *years,* you *wait* . . . and . . . what's she going to think of me?

Dunyasha: And I feel like I'm going to faint. I *am* fainting . . .

*Sound. Carriages driving up—***Firs** *hurries across stage. Voice offstage: "In here." Enter—***Charlotta, Varya, Simeonov-Pishchik, Lopakhin, Dunyasha, Servants.**

Anya: Mama.

Lyubov: Yes.

Anya *(pointing to nursery)*: Do you remember this?

Lyubov: Yes.

Varya: My hands are frozen— (*To* **Lyubov:**) Do you see? It's not changed—your room's just the . . . Mama. . . ?

Lyubov: This is where I . . . when I was a little girl I slept here. And now . . . and I'm still like a little girl . . . and *Varya's* still the same . . . my *convent* girl . . . and *Dunyasha* . . .

Gaev: . . . And the *train* . . . and the *train* was two hours late . . . I *ask* you . . . what kind of a way is *that* to. . . ?

Charlotta: My dog has the gout.

Pishchik: He . . . *really.* . . ?

Exit all except **Anya** *and* **Dunyasha.**

Dunyasha: We almost got tired of waiting.

Anya: Four days on this train. I didn't sleep a bit. Oh God I'm cold . . .

Dunyasha (*simultaneously with "cold"*): And when you left—snow on the ground, frost on the ground . . . now, now, but now. (*Pause.*) You left, it was Lent. And here you are—and we *waited* . . . oh, just *kiss* me . . . my little darling . . . how we . . . And do you know. What could you possibly think of this: Yepikhodov, Semyon Panteleevich proposed to me.

Anya: It's always something . . . (*Straightening hair.*) I've lost all my hairpins.

Dunyasha: And he loves me. Can you . . . I . . . what can you think of such a . . .

Anya: *My* room. Just as if I didn't leave. And tomorrow I'll run into the *garden*. Walk in the *trees* . . . how I wish I could just, we didn't sleep the whole way. Now I'm . . .

10

Dunyasha: And you'll never guess who's here? Guess who do you think's come to see us? Petr Sergeich.

Anya: Petya!

Dunyasha: He's living in the boat house. He—

Varya (*entering*): Dunyasha.

Dunyasha: —wanted to come in but we told him to wait 'til morning . . .

Varya: Dunyasha. May we have some coffee please? Mama . . .

Dunyasha: Immediately (*Exits.*)

Varya (*pause*): Thank God you're home. Thank God we're all together. And my little angel has come home.

Anya: Home from the Wars.

Varya: I can imagine.

Anya: Left in Holy Week. So cold. Charlotta talking the whole way—doing her *card* tricks . . . why did you stick me with her. . . ?

Varya: What were you going to, go *alone*? At seventeen. . . ?

Anya: We got to Paris. Cold. Still cold. My French is terrible. And Mama's living in some sixth floor . . . *I*

don't . . . full of French . . . men, ladies, someone
with a book . . . smoke . . . it was so close—and I
hugged her . . . "Mama"—I thought . . . I couldn't let
her go . . .

Varya (*simultaneously with "go"*): Shhhh.

Anya: I felt so *sorry* for her . . .

Varya: Shhhh.

Anya (*simultaneously with "shhhh"*): And she's already
sold the house at Mentone—and she has nothing left.
Nothing—*no* money—and I arrive without a sou . . .
she does not understand. We're at the station restaurant—she orders *everything of such magnitude* . . .
tips them all a *ruble* . . . Charlotta . . . then Yasha
wants another . . . Yasha . . . her new . . . Her
"footman" . . .

Varya: I saw him.

Anya: Then you know what I mean. (*Pause.*) Fine.
(*Pause.*) Then tell me: have they paid the interest?

Varya: What *can* you mean?

Anya: Oh my God—

Varya: In August the whole place will be sold.

Anya: Oh my God . . .

Lopakhin (*looks in and growls like a bear*): Grrrrrrr!!!

Varya: Oh, why don't you just . . . (*He exits.*)

Anya: *Varya*. (*Pause.*) Did he propose? (**Varya** *indicates* "*no*.") Why not? (**Varya** *shrugs shoulders.*) He *loves* you . . . why don't you . . . what are you waiting for?

Varya: I . . .

Anya: What?

Varya: I . . . you know . . . I think . . . I think it's not meant to be—that's what I think and God bless him—it's . . . now I hate to *see* him—everyone talks of our wedding . . . they're always *congratulating* us . . . But—no one's said anything . . . it's like a dream. Running uphi . . . (*Of brooch.*) Oh, look at this—this is *magnificent*.

Anya: Mama bought it. And in Paris I went up in a balloon.

Varya: No!

Anya: Yes, I . . .

Varya: Oh, my *darling*. You're *back* . . . (**Dunyasha** *enters with coffee.*) And do you know all day what I think about? I'm doing the housekeeping and I'm thinking about *you*. We'll marry you off to a rich man—we'll be well-off . . . I'll go on a *retreat*, you

13

know? I'll—then I'll go to *Moscow*, Kiev . . . a *pilgrimage. Holy* . . . and I would walk in holy places.

Yasha (*entering*): Excuse me but may I be permitted to walk through here?

Dunyasha: "May you" . . . Don't you know who I . . . ? *Yasha* . . . ? What did they do to you in Europe . . . ?

(*Pause.*)

Yasha: Who are you?

Dunyasha: Who am . . . ? *Dunyasha*. Feyodor Kosedov's daughter. When you left I was this . . .

Yasha (*embracing her*): Commere . . . (*Gooses her. She screams and drops a dish.*)

Varya: What's going on?

Dunyasha: I broke a plate.

Varya: That's good luck.

Anya: Does Mama know Petya is here?

Varya: No—we'll wake him up later.

Anya: Is it a good thing he's here?

Varya: I . . . ?

Anya: He'll remind her of Grisha. (*Pause.*)

Varya: Six years dead. (*Pause.*)

Anya: Such a pretty boy.

Varya: An angel he was. Like you.

Anya: Petya's going to remind her of him.

Varya: She . . .

Firs (*entering*): The lady wishes *coffee* . . . May we inquire after the *coffee?* (*Sees coffee.*) *Yes.* And the *cream* for the . . .

Dunyasha (*Remembers the cream. Runs off*): Oh my God . . .

Firs: I should *say.* (**Dunyasha** *exits. To himself:*) All in the preparation. Back from *Paris.* Back from *abroad.* Once *again.* As many times the *master* would come back from *Paris.* Rolling up the *drive.* Matched horses.

Varya: *Firs.* (*Pause.*)

Firs: Please?

Varya: What are you talking about?

Firs: I have waited and the Lord has *blessed* my waiting for the mistress has *arrived* and I can *die.*

Enter **Lyubov, Gaev, Pishchik, Gaev** *miming billiards.*

Gaev: *Smack.*

Lyubov: "Smack." Let me see! Two cushions, *off the rail* leave it on the long rail.

Gaev: If you can . . . if you can shoot off the rail. Once! *Once*—long ago. Once long ago we slept in this same room. My sister and I. You and I. And now! Now . . . strange as it seems—*unaccountably*—I have grown *old*, the . . .

Lopakhin: Time flies.

Gaev: I . . .

Lopakhin: What?

Gaev: I'm sorry.

Lopakhin: I remarked time flies—

Gaev: Time flies and it still smells of patchouli in this room . . .

Anya: I'm going to bed. Mama—good night.

Lyubov: My wondrous beauty. My angel child—are you glad to be home? I still can't . . . it means nothing to me.

Anya (*kisses* **Gaev**): Uncle . . .

Gaev: God bless you, my darling. You are . . . to me, you are your mother. (*To* **Lyubov**:) *Lyuba:* at her age you looked exactly like this . . . Do you. . . ?

Anya *exits*.

Lyubov: She's just exhausted.

Pishchik: Well, I'd say *so*, after that *trip*, after . . .

Varya: Gentlemen: It's past two. Shall we fold our tents and . . .

Lyubov: Oh, Varya, you haven't changed (*kisses her*)—alright. I'll drink my coffee, then we'll all . . . (**Firs** *puts cushion under her feet*.) Bless you. I've gotten so used to *coffee*. In Paris I drink it day and night . . . (**Firs** *gives her coffee*.) Thank you.

Varya: I'm going to see about the bags. (*Exits*.)

Pause.

Lyubov: Now. Can I be sitting here? Can I be sitting in this room? Can I be home? And if home then why am I sitting here, and why did I sit in a *train* for four days—*weeping* all across this beautiful land; *weeping* while I . . . (*Pause*.) But what is it that one must *do* in life? . . . One must drink one's coffee. (*Pause*.) Which you have gotten and for which I thank you. My dear old man. I am so glad you are still alive.

Anton Chekhov

Firs: Yesterday morning.

Gaev: Glad to hear it.

Lopakhin: Well. I'm off. I have to, five o'clock, I'm going to Kharkov—wanted to stop by—I simply wanted to pay my respects to a magnificent—

Pishchik: . . . And even prettier since her return from Paris—dressed in the latest . . .

Lopakhin (*simultaneously with "latest"*): Your brother, Leonid Andreevich. He said of me this: I am a *lout*—I am a *peasant* . . . this is fine, it means nothing to me—my only wish is that you trust me, as you've always done, that you . . . my dearest lady—my father served your father and grandfather—you, *personally* did something for me once that, through the years, my only thought was that some day I might be blessed . . . blessed with the opportunity to repay, to *show* you some of the great . . . some . . . my feeling for you is, as if it were, as . . . as if you were a blood relation . . . *closer*, as . . .

Lyubov (*simultaneously with "as," jumping up*): Oh. My *God* you know . . . I . . . feel . . . I feel . . . I feel I'm so happy that I'm going to die. I *cannot believe* I am *home*. My *dresser*—my table . . . my *own books* . . .

Gaev: You know, when you were gone your *nurse* died.

18

Lyubov: Rest in peace. They wrote me . . .

Gaev: They did . . . and. And do you know who else died? Anastasius—and you know who left? What's-his-name, Cross-Eyed left and went to live in town.

Pishchik: My daughter, Dashenka, sends her regards . . .

Lopakhin: I wanted to say something cheery but I have to leave . . . and there's no time for it—so I'll say this right out: As you know on the twenty-second of August your cherry orchard is due to be auctioned off for debt, the debts against you being of . . . Etcetera. This is the fact and what I've come to say . . . I have come to say this: I've found you a way out. Here it is—and here's my plan for you: your estate's twenty-five kilometers from the town. And what is at the town? The railroad. Now: your land along the river—break it into lots—and you build summer cottages—you don't even have to sell them. You just rent them out. Each summer *minimum* twenty-five thousand rubles as income from the . . .

Gaev: Excuse me, excuse me, but will you stop talking drivel.

Lyubov (*simultaneously with "drivel"*): Yermolay Alexeevich: I . . . I . . . don't . . . I'm sure I don't understand you.

Lopakhin: You. Rent. Out. The. Cottages which you have built . . . (*Pause.*) Now: the *very least*—one

19

acre, twenty-five rubles—rent them at that price and I *assure* you, by fall, *not one plot*—you won't have one plot left. You'll rent them all—which is to say one thing, and that's congratulations—I congratulate you because you are saved—fine land. Deep river, put in a sand beach . . . and what it is is *strikingly* perfect. Alright? You clear the land, the old buildings, the house will have to come down, but it's served its turn . . . Yes? You cut down the *cherry* orchard . . .

Lyubov: Cut . . . excuse me . . . cut. . . ? (*Pause.*) "We'll have to cut down" . . . If I may, in this whole *"province,"* I cannot think of . . .

Gaev: . . . Sister . . .

Lyubov: It's alright . . . *what* is there? The one thing of note happens to be our cherry orchard.

Lopakhin: It's . . . no, no . . . all that it is is *big*. One crop of cherries every two years. And who buys the crop? *No* one. It rots.

Gaev: *Even* in . . .

Lyubov: . . . It's alright . . .

Gaev: even in the *encyclopaedia*—that—*cherry* orchard . . .

Lopakhin: Fine. But on the twenty-second of August the orchard and this whole estate's going beneath the gavel—Do you see? So, so, so, this is your only . . . I

swear to you—my hand to God; there's no other way!
This is a godsend.

Firs: In my youth. They'd *take* the cherries. *Soak*
them, *marinate* them in . . .

Gaev: Be quiet, Firs—

Firs: Um . . . *casks*. They made preserves. And they,
they also *dried* the cherries and *took* the dried cherries—to Kharkov—to *Moscow*—and sold them. They
had a method of . . . they used to *dry* them . . .

Lyubov: Ah. But where's that method now.

Firs: We have forgotten it.

Pishchik: Madam.

Lyubov: Yes?

Pishchik: In *Paris*. Did you eat frogs?

Lyubov: I ate a crocodile.

Pishchik: *Can* you believe it.

Lopakhin: I want to tell you something: At. One. Time.
What did you have? In this village, in any—Masters,
and, you had peasants. *Now* we have a third class—
cottagers . . . cottage, *cottage* people, renters—*everywhere*. The summer people. *Look* at them—they drink
their tea, they say "How picturesque"—one day,

though, who's to . . . Twenty years from now—he starts out with a garden, and one day, because we win him back to *agriculture,* to the *land* . . . and one day . . . *one* day, your cherry orchard, once again . . .

Gaev: What vicious nonsense you speak.

Enter **Varya** *and* **Yasha**.

Varya: Mamentchka two telegrams for you. (*Hands her telegrams. Goes to wardrobe.*)

Lyubov (*looks*): From Paris— (*Tears them up.*) Paris is over.

Gaev: Lyubov—you know how old this bookcase is?

Lyubov: No.

Gaev: Last week—I pulled out the bottom drawer— what did I find? Burnt in the wood—the date of its manufacture. It was fashioned one hundred years ago . . . can you believe it? If it were a person you would say to celebrate its jubilee—but no. Not, not . . . who'd do it with a book case?

Pishchik: One hundred years. *Think* of it . . .

Gaev: Yes. Isn't that something? (*Pause.*) Most worthy, most esteemed bookcase. (*Pause.*) To you . . . to you, who have, for upwards of *a hundred* years . . . *challenged* us . . . *helped* us. Brought us strength and courage . . . who have nurtured in our family *faith* . . . (*pause*) *faith,* self-knowledge and a . . . (*Pause.*)

Lopakhin: Go on.

Lyubov: Lenya. My dear, you haven't changed.

Gaev: Just just just freeze it on the rail.

Lopakhin: Well. I must leave—I have to go.

Yasha (*simultaneously with* "*go*"): Madam, if you'll permit me. Now is the time set out to take your pill.

Pishchik: *Don't touch that. Please* don't let me see you, my most esteemed, swallowing those . . . what are you going to find in pills? No good, no harm—I commandeer them. (*Takes pillbox, shakes pills into palm, blows on them, puts in mouth, washes down with kvass.*)

Lyubov: Are you . . . are . . . excuse me, are you *mad?*

Pishchik (*simultaneously with* "*mad*"): I swallowed all the pills.

Lopakhin: You could have left some for the rest of us . . .

Firs: In holy week at our place one man ate a whole half barrel of cucumbers.

Lyubov: What *is* he talking about?

Varya: He's been like that for three years. We don't notice it anymore.

Yasha (*simultaneously with "any"*): . . . declining years.

(**Charlotta** *in white dress, thin, tight corset, with lorgnette at her belt, she enters.*)

Lopakhin: Ah. Ah. Charlotta Ivanovna, and I haven't welcomed you back yet.

Charlotta: Yes. Yes. You kiss the hand. And tomorrow the elbow . . . and *then* what?

Lopakhin: No luck. No luck in anything today. Charlotta *Ivanovna* . . . eh? What about a trick.

Charlotta: I think not. If you will excuse me . . . (*Exits.*)

Lopakhin: Alright. Yes. In three weeks then. Madam. (*Kisses* **Lyubov's** *hand.*) Until then. (*To* **Gaev:**) Sir—goodbye . . .

Gaev: —goodbye.

Lopakhin (*to* **Pishchik**): Goodbye . . . (*To* **Gaev:**) . . . I don't feel like going. (*To* **Lyubov:**) If you should change your mind about the cottages—just let me know, and I'll get you fifty-thousand as a loan. Like *that*. Let me know. Seriously, *please* . . .

Varya: *"Please"—please*, will you get out. . . ?

Lopakhin: I'm going . . . (*Exits.*)

Gaev: What a bore. Ah. Ah . . . I bite my tongue. I beg your *pardon*. *Varya*, speaking of your fiancé, in such . . .

Varya: . . . Uncle, let's just . . .

Lyubov: There's no need to be—we're all glad for you. *Varya*. We are. He's a good *man*, he's . . .

Pishchik: A man should speak only the quantifiable truth. My Dashenka says. She says many things. (*Snores but immediately wakes up*.) All the same— madam—I'm forced to ask you for a loan of two hundred forty rubles—*tomorrow* I must pay the interest on my mortgage.

Varya (*simultaneously with "mortgage"*): We don't have it.

Lyubov: In point of fact, I have nothing—

Pishchik: Waaal . . . I'll get it somehow—I never lose hope—you know—one day I'm ruined. The next day—you remember? They routed the railroad through my land . . . and *boom*. If not today tomor- row—Dashenka's bought a lottery ticket—first prize—two . . . mind you . . . *two hundred* thousand rubles.

Lyubov: Well. Our coffee's drunk and we should go to bed.

Firs (*brushing* **Gaev's** *clothes, reprovingly*): Not . . .

not the trousers to this suit—what am I going to do with you. . . ?

Varya: Anya's asleep. (*Opens window.*) Well, look: the sun is up. It's not cold—look . . . Mamentchka . . . most beautiful trees . . .the air . . . the starlings are out . . .

Gaev (*sighs*): The orchard is all white. Lyuba—(*pause*) our long avenue—straight as a rope—shining on moonlit nights. Do you remember? Lyuba?

Lyubov: Oh God, my childhood. So pure. Slept in the same room. Sainted room. Every morning felt the same. I woke in happiness to look out . . . *just* like this. Nothing has changed. "Oh my pure orchard white." After dark autumn weather, after cold weather—young again—and full of happiness again your spirits have not left you. But I cannot lift from my heart . . . from my shoulders that stone which I bear, and let the past . . .

Gaev: . . . and how odd. That they're going to sell our cherry orchard to pay "debts."

Lyubov: I see. My sainted mother. Walking in her orchard in a white . . . I see her.

Gaev: Where?

Varya (*simultaneously with "where"*): God be with you. Mamentchka.

Lyubov: There's no one there. It just looked—for a moment—by the summerhouse. For a moment—a white tree . . .

Enter **Trofimov.**

Lyubov: My orchard. White against blue.

Trofimov: Lyubov Andreevna—just came by to welcome you home. Now I'll—I was ordered to wait til morning, but I didn't have the patience. (*Pause.*)

Varya: It's Petya Trofimov.

Trofimov: Petya Trofimov. Grisha's, rest in peace . . . Grisha's (*Pause*) Grisha's tutor. (*Pause.*) Am I so changed?

Lyubov *embraces him, crying quietly.*

Gaev: Yes. Alright. Enough, Lyuba—enough.

Varya: Petya. I *pleaded* with you to wait til tomorrow . . .

Lyubov: Grisha . . . my Grisha . . . my son . . .

Varya: Mama—it was God's will—

Trofimov *sighs.*

Lyubov: And drowned. And dead for what? For what, my friend? *For what?* And my Anya asleep and I'm shouting . . . (*Pause.*) Petya . . . what's happened to you? You've grown so *old* . . .

Trofimov: On the train—a woman called me "shabby gentleman"—

Lyubov: You were a *boy*—you were our dear little student—now—you're losing your *hair—eyeglasses* . . . what's happened to our student?

Trofimov: I am still . . . a student. I will always be a student—

Lyubov *kisses* **Gaev,** *then* **Varya.**

Lyubov: Well. (*Pause.*) Enough. We all need sleep. *Leonid*—you've gotten older, too.

Pishchik: Yes. Yes. "You go to sleep, too"—I'll stay here tonight, if I. And tomorrow, Lyubov Andreevna—*dear,* if I may . . . I *must* ask just two hundred forty rubles . . .

Gaev (*simultaneously with "rubles"*): My God, that's all my money in the world.

Pishchik: . . . to pay the interest on my mortgage.

Lyubov: My dear man—I have no money.

Pishchik: . . . which, of course, I will repay. A trifling sum . . . if . . .

Lyubov: Yes. Yes. Alright. Leonid will get it . . . give it to him Leonid.

Gaev: I think not.

Lyubov: He'll pay it back . . . he *needs* it. *Give* it to him.

Lyubov, Trofimov, Pishchik, *and* **Firs,** *exit.* **Gaev, Varya and Yasha** *remain.*

Gaev: My sister has not yet disabused herself of the ways of the rich. (*To* **Yasha:**) My friend, excuse me, please, you smell of broiled chicken.

Yasha: Leonid Andreevich. *You* haven't changed your ways either.

Gaev: *What?* What did he say?

Varya (*simultaneously with "he"*): *Yasha.* Your mother's been here since yesterday. Waiting here. Sitting in the servants quarters, waiting for you.

Yasha: God reward her trials.

Varya: Have you no shame?

Yasha: Tell her to come back tomorrow. (*Exits.*)

Varya: Mamentchka isn't changed. She'd still give away everything she owns—

Gaev (*pause*): When many remedies are proposed for
a disease that means the disease is incurable. I *think*. I
plan. I rack my *brains* . . . I have so many schemes
. . . ideas . . . it would be good if we . . . (*pause*) if
someone left us *money*. It would be good if *Anya* married a very wealthy man—it would be good to go to
Yaroslavl once again, and try our luck with our rich
aunt . . . who is so *very* rich.

Varya: . . . if God would help us.

Gaev: No, don't cry. Who is so very, but does not ap-
prove of us. Because our sister married an attorney
instead of a nobleman. (**Anya** *appears, unseen by*
Gaev.) Because my *sister* married a commoner and
then proceeded to *comport* herself—we can't say very
virtuously, can we? No. But who is, withal . . . but
whom I love. My glorious sister. Of whom we must
say, with all the mercy in the world . . . comports herself—*wantonly, viciously* . . . in whose every act we
must say, we find depraved and . . .

Varya: Anya's in the door.

Gaev: . . . and quite annoying speck in my right eye.
Your *vision* worsens—your eyes tear. I'm in the village court last Wednesday, and . . .

Enter **Anya.**

Varya: Why aren't you sleeping, dear?

Anya: I don't feel like sleeping. I can't sleep.

Gaev (*kisses her*)**:** My darling. My niece, my angel—you are not my niece, you are my . . . believe me, my radiant . . .

Anya: I do believe you, Uncle. I. But why do you, why must you . . . Why do you speak of Mama that way? Your *sister*. Why . . .

Gaev: Yes, I know. I know. It's . . . there's no. It's inexcuseable; and I *did* it. I *did* it. And when I was done I *knew*.

Varya: Then, Uncle. What she, what she says is . . . We should *all* be . . .

Anya: *All* of us could be happier, if you would hold your tongue.

Gaev: I *will* hold it. I *do*. I am still—and I'll tell you what *else:* Last *Wednesday?* At the Bank! We were talking and it *seems* . . . It *seems* that it *may be possible* to get . . . as you know . . . to get a *promissory* note, to sign for a loan and, so pay our interest to the bank.

Varya: Pray God to help us.

Gaev: And Tuesday he said come and ask again. It all will . . . (*To* **Anya:**) Your Mama will speak to Lopakhin, who, as you see, who will refuse her *nothing*— We'll, when you are rested you'll go see your Grandmother in Yaroslavl. *So* we have: *Lopakhin, Grandmother,* a promissory . . . A three-pronged attack. I say: How can it fail? As a three-fold bond is not soon . . . By . . . by . . . by . . . I swear by anything you like: The estate *shall* . . . shall not be sold. I swear it on my hope of happiness. My word on it. Shake hands. It shall not go to auction, or call me . . . call me . . . call me dishonorable call me . . . By the stars and sun and on my soul. It shall not . . . I swear before God.

Anya: Uncle.

Gaev: I swear it before God.

Anya: Oh what a good man you are.

Firs (*entering*): Leonid Andreevich, do you fear *nothing? Go to sleep.*

Gaev: Yes. Yes. Right now. Yes. I'm fine. I'll do for myself. Goodnight. Messieurdames, adieu! *Tomorrow* everything comes *right, tonight:* sleep. (*Pause.*) I am a person of the '80s. Who praises that time? No one. But I *lived* in it. And gained convictions. And suffered for them. And not for nothing does the peasant love me. Why? I know his ways. I know him when he's . . .

Anya: Uncle.

Varya: Uncle, goodnight.

Firs: Leonid—

Gaev: Yes. Yes. Yes. Alright. No shot. No shot at all. What does he do? Force-follow on the rail. *Impossible.* Plenty of *chalk*, though, and . . .

Gaev *exits with* **Firs.**

Anya: Oh, I feel better. I don't feel like going to Grandmother, but when we . . . He's right. We must . . . Uncle, you're right. If we *act*, then we feel . . .

Varya: We must sleep and I'm going to leave you. When you were gone, you know, *unrest* . . . there . . . The, the old servants quarters. Polya, *Yestignei,* they, evenings they would let the young ones in to *drink* . . . to . . . I said nothing. Then I hear they're spreading *rumours*. How *hard* I am. How I ordered they were to only eat *peas*—"How stingy she is . . ." Oh? Alright. I think, if that's the way it is. I called Yestignei—he comes, "How do you do?" I say, "Yestignei . . . you're a damn *fool*. You're not acting in your own best . . ." (*Pause.*) Anya? (*Pause.*) Anya . . . Come on my darling we are going to bed. Come on.

Trofimov *enters.*

She's asleep.

Anya: I'm not tired. Do you hear the bells. . . ? Mama? Uncle. . . ? I left them at my . . .

Varya: Shh. Shh. Angel. Here we go . . .

Varya *leads* **Anya** *off.*

Trofimov: My springtime. My dear morning sun.

Act Two

A field. The sun will soon be down. **Charlotta, Yasha** *and* **Dunyasha** *are sitting on the bench:* **Epihodoff** *is standing near and playing the guitar.* **Charlotta** *has taken a rifle from off her shoulders and is adjusting the buckle on the strap.*

Charlotta: As I don't have a passport how old can I be? Who knows. *As a child* we travelled to fairs and we performed the *Leap for Life.* The carnival—various feats man has performed down through time. (*Pause.*) Mama died. My father met a certain German lady who taught me excellent well. Then I became a governess. Where do I come from? What is this? A *mystery?* Who were my parents? Were they married. . . ? Ah. (*Eats cucumber.*) I. Don't. Know. Everyone loves suspense. But don't ask me. When you feel like talking. Who can you talk to? Yes? "Everyone has someone . . ."? I must beg to differ.

Yepikhodov (*playing and singing*):
"Yes I care nothing for this world of woe
A friend

A foe
An empty show . . . I pray that love would lift my soul
and grace my life but no."
What in the world is better than to play
the mandolin?

Dunyasha: That's a guitar.

Yepikhodov: To a madman in love it's a mandolin.
(*Sings.*) ". . . I pray that love would lift my soul and
grace my life but *no* . . ."

(**Yasha** *joins him and they sing together.*)

Charlotta: These people sing like swine.

Dunyasha (*To* **Yasha**): No. Why should you go
abroad? What do they have *there?*

Yasha: If you don't know you don't know . . . (*Yawning and then lighting a cigar.*)

Yepikhodov: *Abroad* it's finished. It's a jigsaw puzzle.
Filled in. Everything's set.

Yasha: . . . is that a fact?

Yepikhodov: I'm a thoughtful person. Well-read . . .
Many, many books . . . You read them. You think . . .
Here's what I can't understand: Do I want to live? . . . or
do I . . . this is the problem. To *live,* or *shoot* myself—
which is why I'm never without my revolver. (*Showing a
revolver.*) This one before me now.

Charlotta: Well—that's enough of *this*—goodbye—
Yepikhodov you are a thoughtful man . . .

Yepikhodov: Thank you.

Charlotta: And yet you burn with passion too . . . *How*
the girls must adore you. How they must . . . And I,
although, *alone* forlorn, no family—No . . . who knows
who I am? The North *Wind?* I doubt it sincerely . . .
quite alone . . . Goodnight, goodnight. (*Exits.*)

Yepikhodov (*pause*): to . . . as we were? . . . The sub-
ject under our discussion . . . *fate* . . . (*Pause.*) Fate
tosses me as a small ship on the sea of . . . that's suffi-
cient. This morning: I wake out of a morning sleep—
what do I see? A *spider* on my chest—I promise you.
Eh? Then what of it? Take a glass of kvass—what's
in the bottom of it? A *cockroach*. Hah. Avdotea
Feodorovna. May we . . . I'd, could I have one word
with you?

Dunyasha: Yes.

Yepikhodov (*pause*): Alone?

Dunyasha (*sighs*): Alright. Alright. Get me my, but
get me, my scarf, will you. By the door. It's getting . . .

Yasha: "Endless Misfortune." Between you and
me . . .

Yepikhodov: Yes Ma'am. Yes I will. Yes I will . . . and
now: Where's my revolver . . . (*Exits.*)

Dunyasha: Pray God he doesn't shoot himself. (*Pause.*) When I was a girl I was happy. Now I'm always worrying. I'm always anxious. When I was a girl they took me to live with gentlefolk. My hands are white . . . I'm soft . . . I am afraid of my shadow. And if you deceive me *Yasha*—then I don't know what I'll do.

Yasha: My little cabbage—and you're right—a girl loses her reputation, what *is* she?

Dunyasha: I'm desperately in love with you. You're fine, you're *travelled* . . .

Yasha: Yes, I am—I'll tell you a girl falls in love, she's like a pig. To smoke alone in the fresh air however . . . Ah . . . Ah . . . It's the Masters! (**Dunyasha** *embraces him.*) No, no, get on home. Go home, go as if you're coming from the river. You want them to think I'm *meeting* you. . . ?

Dunyasha: Your cigar gives me a . . . headache . . . (*With a cough. Goes out.*)

Lopakhin: *Decide. Decide. Decide.* There is no *question. Yes* or *no*. The cottage or the auction block. One word. Yes, or no.

Lyubov (*simultaneously with* "*no*"): *Who* has been smoking . . . Who has been *smoking?* Those *vile* cigars?

Gaev (*simultaneously with "cigars"*): You build a railway. What was long has been made short— Ride into town for breakfast? Yes, why not? Hand me the bridge. Right English takes it to the left. May I go back for one quick game?

Lyubov: Later.

Lopakhin: *Madam*—one word— Your answer?

Gaev (*absently*): One word . . .

Lyubov (*looking in her purse*): Yesterday this was full of money. Today, almost gone. Varya: "Economize: feed them on carrot soup—" In the kitchen all the old men get is *peas*. And me, I squander it (*drops purse*). There you are—*scattered*.

Yasha: If madam permits? (*He stoops to pick up her purse.*)

Lyubov: *Thank* you, Yasha. And why do we go out? Out to this *restaurant*—loud music, bad food—reeks of disinfectant . . . And *you*. Eat too much. *Talk* too much—he talks to the waiters about the "*contract social*" . . .

Gaev: I should shut up.

Lopakhin: I . . .

Gaev: . . . I am incorrigible. (*To* **Yasha:**) What are you dancing about?

Yasha: You fill me with glee.

Gaev: This man must go. If he stays—

Lyubov: Leave—Yasha. Leave us.

Yasha: Madam, at *once*.

Lopakhin: Deriganov's coming to bid on your estate. And if he wants it he'll get it.

Lyubov: Who says he's coming to bid?

Lopakhin: They're saying it in town.

Gaev: Our aunt has promised to send something down.

Lopakhin: . . . she has.

Gaev: But how much and when that is a mystery.

Lopakhin: Yes—but. . . ? How much? One hundred thousand. . . ? Two?

Lyubov: If she sends ten or fifteen we'd be very grateful—

Lopakhin: I have never seen your like—my *friends*. Ten or fifteen. . . ! I tell you in plain words your estate will be sold. What do you . . . don't you *understand?*

40

Lyubov: Then what are we to do? Teach us.

Lopakhin: Teach. Yes I teach you every day. Every day: I say the same thing. One thing. The cherry orchard and the land must be leased out for cottages. It must be done *quickly*. It must be done right now or the land will be auctioned. Act—and say yes to the cottages and you'll have as much money as you like. You will be saved. That's what I say.

Gaev: And that's it.

Lopakhin: What am I to do? *Faint?* Spit *blood?* Climb a *tree* . . . you *kill* me, you're *killing* me . . . you old *woman,* you . . .

Gaev: I. What?

Lopakhin: Old *woman.* You heard me . . . *(Starts to exit.)*

Lyubov: No. No. No. Please don't go . . . my friend. My dear friend. I beg you. *Please.* And we will think of something.

Lopakhin: What is there to think of?

Lyubov: Please don't go. Please. Please. I wish . . . *All the time* I feel a *weight* above my head . . . you . . . but when you're here . . .

Gaev *(to himself):* . . . Or *two* rails—two rails, back to the center . . .

41

Lyubov (*simultaneously with "center"*): We have sinned so much . . .

Lopakhin: *How* have you sinned?

Gaev (*simultaneously with "sinned"*): They tell me I spent my whole fortune on fruit drops.

Lyubov: How have I? I have always wasted money—squandered it—like an insane—married a man who only produced debts. Who died of drink. Who died of champagne—and then I met another, and became . . . and fell in love with him. And because of that my boy died. In this river—drowned—and I left. Never coming home. Abroad. To escape. The man pursued me. Mercilessly. I bought a cottage near Menton. And he came and was taken sick and for three years I nursed him. Not knowing rest day or night. He baked the spirit out of me. My cottage was sold for his debts. I went to Paris. There he left me for a younger girl. (*Pause.*) And I tried to kill myself, and . . . and longed for Russia. For my home. For my little girl, I longed . . . Lord. Forgive my sins. And cease to punish me. And today, yes (*takes telegram out of pocket*): a telegram from Paris—he "Begs my friendship and entreats me to return . . ." (*Listens.*) What do I hear?

Gaev: Our celebrated Jewish orchestra.

Lyubov: They're still here?

Gaev: Yes.

Lyubov: We should, you know, we should arrange an evening—

Lopakhin (*listening*): I can't . . . "And step . . . and step . . . and play the fool for German money . . ." You know I was at the theatre last night, a . . . *very* funny . . .

Lyubov: Yes, yes, what? What was so funny? Plays. We look at plays . . . we should look at ourselves. You all should look more often at yourselves. How *shabbily* we live . . . the *things* we say . . . the *nonsense* we . . .

Lopakhin: You're absolutely right. You say it right out and you're right. Our life is *stupid*. My father beat me— a *peasant*—a *stupid*—*understood* nothing . . . *knew* nothing . . . lived life like a pig . . . a . . . (*Pause.*) And I *am* my father . . . my, uh . . . my . . . *handwriting* is illegible . . . my . . . (*Pause.*) I . . .

Lyubov: It's time you married.

Lopakhin: Yes, that's absolutely true.

Lyubov: To our Varya. To our fine Varya.

Lopakhin (*simultaneously with "Varya"*): Yes . . .

Lyubov: A simple girl—a fine girl . . . works all day— *adores* you . . . and I know you've—I know that you've "fancied" her a long while. Isn't that true now? (*Pause.*)

Lopakhin: Why not. (*Pause.*) Alright—I have no objection. She's a nice . . . she's a nice girl . . .

Gaev: They offered me a place . . . at the bank. Did I say? Six thousand a year.

Lyubov: What?

Firs: Sir. Your overcoat. Please put it on, as it's becoming damp.

Gaev: Give it to me.

Firs: I'll give it to you—but you went off this morning *without* it . . .

Lyubov: Firs. You've grown old.

Firs: Madame?

Lopakhin: They're saying that you've grown very old.

Firs: I've been alive a long time. They were going to marry me off, your papa was not yet in the world. The Liberation came. I was already grown old in the service. I accepted freedom. "Masters," I said . . . I remember. Everyone was happy. So happy—for what? What were they so happy for?

Lopakhin: That's right. We've lost so much. We've given up *flogging* . . .

Firs: That's it. At one time—the masters had their places. Peasants had their own. Now what do you have? Nothing. You can't know anything.

Gaev: Shut up, Firs. Tomorrow. I'm going into town—I've got a meeting with a general who may co-sign my note.

Lopakhin: I don't *think* so. And I don't think that you're going to pay the interest.

Trofimov, Anya, *and* **Varya** *enter.*

Gaev: Our little ones—

Anya: Mama.

Lyubov: My darlings. My very own. How I adore you. Come here—sit by me.

Lopakhin: Our eternal student—studying the feminine sex.

Trofimov: Why don't you mind your own affairs?

Lopakhin (*simultaneously with "affairs"*): Almost fifty: But still a student, though. . . !

Trofimov: Why don't you just . . .

Lopakhin: Ah. Ah. Eccentric one—losing your temper?

Anton Chekhov

Trofimov: Why don't you stop goading me.

Lopakhin: Alright. I will. I will. Student. Study *me*—tell me *this*—Who am I?

Trofimov: You're a rich man. You'll soon be a millionare. In *life* we have both predators and *prey*. And both it seems, are necessary. For both exist. *You*, you are the *predator* who . . . (*Pause.*)

Lopakhin: I'm listening.

Trofimov: Who preys on . . .

Varya: *Petya* . . . tell us about *astronomy*.

Lyubov: —No, I know. Let us continue yesterday's inquiry.

Trofimov: And that was?

Gaev: The proud man.

Pause.

Trofimov: Yesterday. (*Pause.*) What did we discuss yesterday? For we spoke and arrived at nothing. "The Proud Man." In the proud man—in *pride* as you have it—we see something mystical. We see what we would term "accomplishment." But if you look at the man you see a person *unintelligent—self-involved*, therefore *coarse*, therefore unhappy . . . is this man to

46

be admired? We are left with *this* . . . (*Pause.*) What is it one must *do*, in life? *Work* . . . for the . . .

Gaev: All the same, you die—

Trofimov: And what does this mean? And who knows you die? Perhaps man has a hundred senses and at death only the five we know expire—and ninety-five remain.

Lyubov: What a beautiful thought.

Lopakhin: Stunning. A lovely thought.

Trofimov: . . . And mankind goes forward—man goes forward—perfecting its powers, its mastery . . . and what was unattainable becomes . . . becomes *real.* For him who only *works*—who *works.* Who lends his powers to those who seek the truth. Who, who . . . and the intelligentsia—they save nothing—they do nothing—they profess to live in a world of ideas, they mistreat servants, starve the peasants—they read nothing, *do* nothing . . . they only *"think."* What do they understand? *Art? Science?* Such such such . . . stern faces—serious demeanor . . . they philosophize while before them the workers starve—live life in misery, in filth—in moral . . . (*Pause.*) And, and our *philosophy* is what? A child's toy. A liberal *excuse*— our badge—but where are the day-nurseries about which they talk—and . . . where *are* the reading rooms, the . . . they're in novels . . . in *books* . . . in philosophy. Here there is only filth, barbarity. Philistinism . . . I (*pause*) I . . . there's nothing in idle discourse. I feel that I should stop.

Lopakhin: You know—I get up every morning, five o'clock—I work all day—every day, I handle money— I do *business* . . . *Do* so and you see what mankind *is* in this world—how few honorable men there are. No decency. (*Pause.*) Sometimes when I can't sleep I think "Lord . . . you've given us—vast forests, fields, endless horizons, we . . . to live in them we should be *giants* . . ."

Lyubov: Giants in fairy tales only please.

Anya: Yepikhodov.

Gaev: Ladies and gentlemen—the sun has set.

Trofimov: Yes.

Gaev: Nature—marvelous one—and thou whom we call mother—thou shines all around with inner radiance—with morning—beautiful and yet indifferent—being at once nurture and destruction— being—

Varya: Uncle.

Anya: Uncle, please—

Trofimov: Better "three cushions off the white."

Gaev: Yes. Alright . . . I am silent.

All sit silently, only **Firs** *is heard muttering. Suddenly a sound is heard as if from the sky, like the sound of a snapped string, dying away mournfully.*

Lyubov: What's that?

Lopakhin: I . . . (*Pause.*) A wire snapped—a bucket falling in a mine. (*Pause.*) Far . . .

Gaev: Perhaps a bird of some kind—a "heron."

Trofimov: A horned owl—

Lyubov: It's somehow—

Firs: Just before the catastrophe. There was the same . . . an owl screeched and the samovar whistled all night. With no fire under it. (*Pause.*)

Gaev: What catastrophe?

Firs: The, the Liberation.

Pause.

Lyubov: *Friends.* Evening is falling—shall we . . . (*To* **Anya:**) My darling, what *is* it?

Anya: I'm alright, Mama, it just . . .

Anton Chekhov

Trofimov: Excuse me—who is. . . ?

Stranger (*entering*): Pardon me—would you tell me—please will this road take me to the station?

Gaev: Yes. Just . . . (*Gestures.*)

Stranger: Thank you. I am in your debt. Isn't the weather— (*Pause. Declaims.*)
>"Brother mine,
>Go by the river
>By the flowing Volga
>Go—
>The flowing stream.
>Who's suffering
>So unlike to my own." (*He breaks off.*)

Mademoiselle . . . May a hungry countryman ask thirty kopecks. . . ?

Varya *screams.*

Lopakhin: Get out—Get away—away from here . . .

Lyobov: Here—take it . . . here . . . (*Searches her purse.*) No—I'm. I have no silver. Here. (*She hands him a coin.*)

Anya: *Mama,* not a gold coin.

Stranger: I am eternally in your debt. (*He exits.*)

Varya: Oh my God. I'm going to go . . . Mama—we have nothing to eat at home and you gave him gold?

Lyubov: What's to be done with me? A stupid woman . . . (*To* **Lopakhin:**) Please, please, please. Take over my affairs . . . My banker! I . . . A *loan*.

Lopakhin: Of course—

Lyubov: Let us retire. Messieurdames— It's time. And *Varya*. Here we, all convened, here we stand and felicitate you on your betrothal.

Varya: Mother. That, I don't find amusing.

Lopakhin: "Orelia, get thee to a bakery."

Gaev: You know. *Look* at this: If I don't have my hand around a cue for a while my *hands* shake—

Lopakhin: "Oh nymph. In thine orisons . . ."

Lyubov: My friends . . . Shall we. . . ?

Varya: That man frightened me.

Lopakhin: My last: I beg to *remind* you that on August 22nd the cherry orchard is going to be sold at auction. May I leave you all with that?

Exeunt, save **Anya** *and* **Trofimov.**

Anya: *Thank* you, Stranger—You have frightened Varya off. And now we are alone.

Trofimov: Frightened her. Varya's scared that we will fall in love with each other. You know . . . She won't leave us alone . . . it's funny. (*Pause.*) Some people . . . how little they let themselves understand. Tied down by the illusion of love—and we're above it— how that "weight" prevents their happiness . . . "Love" . . . how it . . . they can't see how . . . it *stays* them . . . from the path of their life. (*Pause.*) But we would rather *walk* that path.

Anya: How beautifully you do speak. (*Pause.*) Isn't it fine today?

Trofimov: Yes. It . . .

Anya (*simultaneously with "it"*): And you know what you have *done* to me. Petya . . . I loved it so dearly . . . our cherry orchard. Our garden. But now . . . somehow it's different and you *speak,* and . . . I cannot love it as before.

Trofimov: All Russia is our garden. Our country is vast and contains many things—if you *reflect*, Anya, your ancestors owned slaves who . . . (*pause*) *worked* the land, pruned the trees. Each tree, every leaf *on* the tree represents their lives. The leaves blow and it is human beings speaking to you—and they're saying they have been deprived . . . and lived to . . . and suffered to create this idyll your family enjoys. You live on credit. You live on the work and off the sufferings of people you would not allow into your home. We are behind the times. Two hundred years. And cannot live in the past and yet we have no plan for the future. We "philosophize," which is to say we *gasp* from too much leisure. Broken free, in order to live in the world, we must atone. (*Pause.*) *First,* to regain that which we have lost. We have lost our place. We must atone. We must atone. We must confess and atone and be *done* with it. Atone by *suffering,* by work—by, only by continual hard labor—do you understand?

Anya: I do.

Trofimov: Show me you understand.

Anya: The house is not my house—and I am leaving it. I swear it.

Trofimov: Throw the keys down the well and walk away.

Anya: How well you said that . . .

Trofimov: Trust in me. Anya, I am not yet thirty. I know I am young, and I am still a student but I have seen much—endured much. Hunger . . . (*Pause.*) Summer and winter . . . I have been sick. Worried . . . wondering . . . (*Pause.*) *Everywhere.* Day and night, I felt it. I . . . and it is coming . . . Throbbing in me— *Happiness.* I *see* it, Anya. (*Pause.*)

Anya: The moon is rising—

Yepikhodov *is heard playing the same sad song on the guitar. Somewhere near the poplars* **Varya** *is looking for* **Anya** *and calls: "Anya where are you?"*

Trofimov: Yes. The moon is rising. And a better time is coming. A happier time. *Nearer, nearer . . .* Perhaps we will live to see it. And if we do not it does not matter. Others will after us.

Varya (*off*): *Anya. Anya!* Where are you?

Trofimov (*sighs*): Oh, Varya . . . Will you please!

Anya: I know! Oh. Oh. Let's go to the river!

Trofimov: Yes. Then, let's go. (*They exit.*)

Varya (*off*): *Anya.* (*Pause.*) Anya!

Act Three

The drawing room, separated by an arch from ball-room. Orchestra playing. Evening. In ballroom, voice of **Pishchik:** *"Promenade a' une paire!" They enter drawing room.* **Pishchik** *shouts "Grand round, bal-ancez!" and "Les cavaliers a'genoux et remerciez vos dames!"* **Firs** *in frock coat goes by with seltzer on tray.* **Pishchik** *and* **Trofimov** *enter drawing room.*

Pishchik: Well, I'm a full-blooded man. Suffered two strokes, and it's hard to dance, but as the man said, "Run with the herd—bark, or don't bark, but wag your tail . . ." My late father, rest in peace, loved to say . . . as he *loved* a joke, this man: "The ancient ignoble clan of Simeonov-Pishchik is lineally de-scended from that very nag Caligula inducted in the Senate." But the *thing* of it, and here's the *thing,* is *this:* no money. Yes. "The hungry dog believes only in meat" . . . (*Pause.*) . . . meat. (*Pause.*) I, uh . . . and so all . . . (*pause*) all . . . The only thought I have is money.

Trofimov: You know, there actually *is* something of the horse about you.

Pishchik: I *said* there was. What about it? Horse is a fine beast . . . You can *sell* a horse—

Varya *appears.*

Trofimov: Madam *Lopakhina* . . . Madam *Lopakhina* . . .

Varya: "The shabby gentlemen."

Trofimov: Proud *of* it.

Varya: Well, we've hired musicians, and I'd like to know what we're going to pay them with . . . (*Exits.*)

Trofimov: You know—if all the effort you've spent scrambling to pay interest—if you'd put this effort into something *meaningful*—you could have moved the earth.

Pishchik: Who are you? Nietzsche? *Nietzsche* . . . a great philosopher, says in his works that it is perfectly permissible to counterfeit bills.

Trofimov: And you've read Nietzsche?

Pishchik: Not exactly. No. But Dashenka was telling it to me— And it fell on receptive ears, because if I don't have three hundred rubles by day-after-tomorrow . . . I have one hundred and thirty already, thank God. (*Feels pocket. Pause.*) I've lost my money. (*Pause.*) Oh, my God . . . where is . . . what am I

going to . . . (*Finds it.*) Ah. Oh, ah, slipped behind
the lining! *Here it* is!! Here it is!!!

Enter **Lyubov** *and* **Charlotta.** **Lyubov** *singing.*

Lyubov: And where in world is Leonid? And what is
he doing in town? Dunyasha . . . give the musicians
some tea.

Trofimov: I will bet that the auction never took place.

Lyubov: And the musicians came late. And . . . Well,
well. Well. Oh, well, what does it matter?

Charlotta (*produces playing cards*): Gentlemen. An
ordinary deck of cards. Think of a card.

Pishchik: I have it.

Charlotta: Shuffle the deck. Hand it to me. Eins,
zwei, drei! Now: Mr. Pishchik . . . feel in your right
pocket. What is there?

Pishchik: A card.

Charlotta: What was the card you thought of?

Pishchik: Eight of spades.

Charlotta: Eight of spades? And what is the card in
your right pocket? (*Takes it out.*) Eight of spades! Ha!
How did you do it? (*Holds cards.*) Hey, presto! (*Does a*

flourish with the deck. To **Trofimov:**) *Quickly,* what is the top card?

Trofimov: I . . . queen of spades.

Charlotta (*turns the top card and hands it to him*): The queen of spades.

Trofimov (*simultaneously with "spades"*): Well I . . .

Charlotta (*to* **Pishchik**): What is the top card?

Pishchik: Ace of hearts.

Charlotta: Pick it up.

Pishchik (*does so*): Ha! (*Shows it.*) Look!

Charlotta (*claps hands—cards disappear*): Lovely weather wouldn't you say?

Mystery voice: *Oh* yes . . . yes.

Charlotta: Excuse me?

Mystery voice: Magnificent weather. *You're* looking well.

Charlotta: I am. *Thank* you.

Mystery voice: Not at all.

Station master: Bravo! Ventriloquista! Bravo.

Pishchik: Charlotta Ivanovna.

Charlotta: What?

Pishchik: I am in love with you.

Charlotta: No thanks—I'll keep my job.

Trofimov (*to* **Pishchik**): You horse. You're such a horse.

Charlotta (*simultaneously with* "*such*"): May I have your attention for a moment please. (*Takes a lap rug from a chair. Pause.*) An oriental rug for sale. What am I bid, please? (*She holds the rug up. Pause.*) No.

Pishchik: I . . .

Charlotta: Going once, going twice. Eins, zwei, drei . . . (*Lowers rug.* **Anya** *appears standing behind it.*)

Lyubov: Bravo! Bravo! (*Applause.*)

Charlotta: And that concludes the . . . No. I beg your pardon. (*Holds up rug again.*) Eins, zwei, drei . . . (*Produces* **Varya**. *Throws rug to* **Pishchik**.) . . . And the rug is yours. (*Runs off to applause.*)

Pishchik: Oh, my devil! Oh! My little *devil!* What a . . . what . . . (*Goes after her.*)

Lyubov: And *still* where is Leonid? What is he . . .

what is he doing in town? It's all, it's all—it's done—
the auction did or did *not* happen. Why does he keep
us in misery?

Varya (*simultaneously with "misery"*): I'm sure that
Uncle bought it. I am absolutely . . .

Trofimov: . . . Oh, yes . . .

Varya: Yes. Grandmother sent him her power of attorney, and so, so that should account for the debt . . .
for . . . *yes* for *Anya*. I'm sure that Uncle has . . .

Lyubov: . . . To—she sent him fifteen-thousand rubles to buy the estate in her name. What is he going
to do with fifteen thousand . . . he can't even pay the
interest . . . oh, today . . . today. I hear the sentence
on my head—

Trofimov (*to* **Varya**): Madam Lopakhin . . .

Varya: And *you*. My ancient scholar. Twice—twice
you've been kicked out of the *university* . . .

Lyubov (*simultaneously with "university"*): *Varya*.
What is the . . . oh ·well . . . *oh* well . . . He teases
you about Lopakhin . . . you tease him . . . you
should *marry* Lopakhin. No one is *forcing* you. But
. . . he's a good man, and . . .

Varya: Absolutely, Mama, I like him . . . yes . . .

Lyubov: Then *do* it. For God's sake . . . why do you
"wait" . . . I don't understand . . .

Varya: I can't make a proposal to myself. Two *years* everyone's been talking to *me*—talking to him—*but he will not speak to me.* He's either silent or he jokes—or he talks about money. Don't you . . . he's not interested in me! And that's the end of it. If I had *money*—if I had a hundred rubles I would chuck it all and leave, I'd go off—I'd go to a *convent.*

Trofimov: "To a nunnery go."

Varya: Do you know? A student should be *kind.* A student should be compassionate. How *ugly* you've grown—you've *aged*—you've *coarsened.*

Yasha (*entering*): Yepikhodov broke the billiard cue.

Varya: Why is he here? Who asked him here? And who is he to play at billiards? I don't understand *any* of you. (*Exits.*)

Lyubov: Please. Don't tease her. Don't you see she's grieving?

Trofimov: Oh yes—I see that—grieving for what? All summer. She's had her nose in my business—following me about—gives me no rest. Gives *Anya* no rest . . . Afraid we'll have a "romance." And what business is it of *hers?* Who had no reason to suspect . . . when I've done nothing. When I have *forsworn* . . . as Anya has done too. Such vulgarity . . . and we are *above* love—

Lyubov: And I am beneath love. Why isn't Leonid . . . is the estate sold or not? How could it be? I . . . I think of it and, *save* me, someone *save* me, someone say something. Speak to me . . . say . . .

Trofimov: It's sold or it's *not* sold. And today we will know. And if yes or no the causes of it are long in the past. It was decided long ago. So be calm. My dear. For once. Look truth in the eye. And be at peace.

Lyubov: What truth? What peace? You see truth and I see *untruth*. I've lost my vision. I see nothing. You—a question presents itself. You *act*, but I say that's be- cause . . . Bec . . . Isn't it because you're *young?* Those questions you decide—you haven't *suffered* them. Not *one*—these . . . "facts" . . . so you look boldly forward. Why? And nothing frightens you. Why? Because life is still hidden from your too— young eyes. (*Pause.*) You are bolder than us. More *honorable*. More . . . Therefore be generous. Be gen- erous to me. Spare me. I was *born* here. My father lived here . . . and my mother. And my grandfather. I love this house. And without my orchard what is my life? And if they must sell it let them sell me too. My darling. (*Embraces him.*) My son drowned here—take pity on me. Good, kind man.

Trofimov: You know you have my sympathy.

Lyubov: Oh, can you say that differently? (*Takes out hankie and telegram falls to the floor.*) My soul is so heavy today. No one can imagine it . . . every sound sends me off. My room is so still, I don't want to go to my room. Petya, do not judge me. I love you. I'd gladly give you Anya in marriage, but but but you must complete your studies. Fate carries you here and there, and . . . you *travel* . . Yes? And you have to do something with your beard . . . what can you do to get it to grow? Oh, my . . .

Trofimov: I have no desire for personal beauty. (*He picks up the telegram from the floor and presents it to her—as if asking her to explain herself.*)

Lyubov: This is a telegram from Paris. I got one yesterday and I got one *today*. And now he's *sick*. Again, and now he's sick, and wants me to, and asks *forgiveness*. And implores me to come back to Paris . . . to stay with him. To—and, and I . . . I *must* . . . (*To* **Petya**.) What are you looking at? Petya—so *stern*. . . ? My dear, what am I going to do. A sick man—alone, unhappy—no one to nurse him, no one to care for him . . . why should I lie about it? I love him. He is a stone around my neck and he will, he will, take me to the bottom. But I cannot live without him. *Petya.* Don't judge me. Don't, don't . . .

Trofimov: I'm sorry, the man robbed you, for God's sake . . .

Lyubov (*covers her ears*): No no no—don't talk that way.

Trofimov: You are the only person . . .

Lyubov: . . . No.

Trofimov: —Yes—in the world who does not know the man's a *thief*, a *liar*, a . . .

Lyubov: *Petya*. You're twenty-six years old, you're just a . . . you're a child, a . . .

Trofimov: So be it.

Lyubov: So be it, yes. Be a man at your age—learn to be a man. It's time you . . . and to understand those who love—and *really* love—and love *yourself*. To *fall* in love, yes! *Don't* dispute me. Yes! *You* have to— what are you? You're like a virgin aunt, a *sissy*—you, what do you mean to . . .

Trofimov: I'm sorry. . . ? What?

Lyubov: "I am above love"—*you* are not above *love*, you—Firs told you, you're a *child*—at *your* age, no lover, no . . .

Trofimov: I'm sorry . . . she's . . . *what* is she saying?

Lyubov: . . . you . . .

Trofimov: *I* won't listen to this . . . it's . . . it's . . . it's . . . everything between us. Is . . . it's *finished*.

Lyubov: Petya—

Trofimov: *No!*

Lyubov: I was . . . *Petya* . . . *Petya* . . . I forgot myself . . . I was *teasing* you. I was just . . . (*He exits.*)

Sound offstage—crash.

Lyubov: What was that?

Anya (*comes in*): Petya fell down the stairs. (*Exits.*)

Pause.

Lyubov: He's . . .

Station master: Excuse me! (*He recites "The Sinner,"
by Tolstoy.*)

*Everyone listens, but he has recited only a few lines
when a waltz is heard. He stops. They all dance. Enter*
Anya, Varya, *and* **Petya.**

Lyubov: *Petya.* (*Pause.*) *Petya* . . . *Oh* . . . pure spirit
. . . spirit of right. (*Pause.*) I ask you to forgive me.
Will you dance with me?

(*She dances with* **Trofimov.** **Anya** *and* **Varya** *dance.*
Firs *enters and leaves cane by door. Enter* **Yasha.**)

Yasha (*of cane*): What's this old man?

Firs: A cane.

Yasha: Why do you have a cane?

Firs: I don't feel well. Generals, Admirals and
Princes—they danced here. Where now we beg the
postmaster to come. I've lived too long. And I am
growing old. The late master, the grandfather. When
we were ill he dosed us all with sealing wax. Whatever

ailed you. (*Pause.*) I've taken sealing wax each morning twenty years. Perhaps more. I think it's kept me alive.

Yasha: Excuse me—you're still alive?

Firs: Play the fool . . .

Trofimov *and* **Lyubov** *dance in ballroom and then in drawing room.*

Lyubov: Merci. I will sit down.

Anya: In the kitchen. A man said the cherry orchard had been sold.

Lyubov: What?

Anya: He said that the cherry orchard had been sold today.

Lyuba: Sold. Sold to whom?

Anya: He didn't say.

Lyubov: Where is this man?

Anya: He left.

Anya *dances with* **Trofimov,** *they pass into ballroom.*

Yasha: Someone's just *saying* that, somebody just . . .

Firs: But Leonid Andreevich is not back. Is he? And he wore his light coat. And now it's turned cold. He'll catch a *chill*, I . . .

Lyubov: I feel I am going to die right now. *Yasha*— go. Find out who said that.

Yasha: She said he left. (*Pause.*)

Lyubov: Firs.

Firs: My lady?

Lyubov: If the estate should be sold, where will you go?

Firs: Where you order me Madam, there I will go.

Lyubov: Are you . . . is something . . . are you ill? You should go to bed.

Firs: Oh yes. Oh yes. I go to bed. And then who serves the *food*—and who looks *after* things—

Yasha: Madame. If I may lay *this* at your feet . . . *should* you return to Paris—would you grant me this? To go with you. For I *cannot* remain here. As you see. Among these "folk"—and this debased *life* of which they're so fond.

Pishchik (*entering*): I beg a boon. A dance . . . one little waltz . . . my most enchanting . . . *two* boons— the *dance* and a hundred-eighty rubles.

Yasha *sings. In ballroom, figure in gray top hat and checked trousers waves hands and jumps.* "Bravo, **Charlotta Ivanovna!**"

Dunyasha: "The young lady *orders* me to dance—I must comply." My head is spinning, my *heart* . . . and just now the postmaster said a thing to me such that . . . took my breath away.

Firs: What did he say.

Dunyasha: He said that I was like a flower.

Yasha: *Tortured* comparison—

Dunyasha: Like a flower. For I am a delicate girl— and I love tender words.

Yepikhodov: You Avdotya Federona—what could one ask from life but that you could not look on me as a bug—

Dunyasha: What. What you. . . ?

Yepikhodov: . . . Although, perhaps I *am* a bug. Perhaps this is the case and I delude myself. And it is the *delusion* which perturbs my thoughts—for I see every day misfortune dogs my steps . . . it's gotten to be an old friend. That I almost smile to see it . . . be that as it may: *Today* I say to you that once you said to me:

Dunuyasha: Can we speak of this later?

Yepikhodov: Yes but—

Dunyasha: No, no. I'm dreaming now.

Yepikhodov (*sighs*): Misfortune every day. *Well.* Then what can one do but *smile?* (*Pause.*) "Hello"— (*Pause.*)

Enter **Varya.**

Varya: Yepikhodov, are you still here? *What* are you doing here? Dunyasha excuse us—you broke the billiard cue—you *roam* the house . . . you're not even *invited* . . .

Yepikhodov: Well. Well. Call me to account. If you think your position warrants, if . . .

Varya: I'm *not* calling you to account—I am *speaking* to you. You wander like a Jew—you do not do your job—it's said we keep a bookkeeper and it is you, but, to "work," as I can see, even . . .

Yepikhodov: What I do with my, *if* I play billiards—a game I adore—or, *whatever* it seems that you see I do. I owe *you* no . . .

Varya: . . . I . . . ?

Yepikhodov: I owe *you* no explanation. What are "*you*"? *You* have no . . .

Varya: You *dare* speak to me that way? Get out of here.

Yepikhodov: I . . .

Varya: Get out of here this *instant,* or I'll have you *thrown* out . . .

Yepikhodov *(pause)*: I, perhaps I spoke too hastily, but isn't there a nicer way to . . .

Varya: *Out.* Get *out! Out.* (*He goes to door, she follows.*) "Endless Misfortune"—go perpetrate it somewhere *else.*

Yepikhodov *(off)*: She has no right to . . .

Varya *(picks up stick)*: Oh *yes? Alright!* (*She swings the stick at the very moment* **Lopakhin** *enters.*)

Lopakhin *enters.* **Varya** *with him. Pause.* **Varya** *hits him with the stick.*

Lopakhin: Sorry to've offended you—

Varya: I . . . oh. Oh I'm so sorry.

Lopakhin: Not at all. We must do it again.

Varya: I didn't hurt you?

Lopakhin: No. I don't think . . . oh.

Varya: What?

Lopakhin: Well, it seems that I . . . have a little *"bump"* . . .

Voices off. "Lopakhin has arrived."

Pishchik: Yes. Yes. You're back . . . *tell* us. You smell of cognac and, we do, too . . . *tell* us.

Lyubov *enters.*

Lyubov: You're back. Where is Leonid?

Lopakhin: We came together—he's coming.

Lyubov: *Well? Well?* The *auction?* What? What? . . . Speak.*

Lopakhin: The auction ended at four. We missed the train back. We had to wait to . . . Nine was . . . I have to sit down.

Gaev *enters.*

Lyubov: *Lenya. Lenya. What?* For God's sake, *quickly* . . .

Gaev (*to* **Firs**): *Firs:* anchovies and kirsch herring—I haven't eaten a thing today—oh, God.

Voice Offstage No. 1:—A carom off the white.

Voice Offstage No. 2: Bravo!

Gaev: Oh God I'm so tired. I'm going to change—Firs!

Gaev *goes to his room.* **Firs** *follows.*

Pishchik: What happened at the auction?

Lyubov: Is the cherry orchard sold?

Lopakhin: Sold.

Lyubov: And who bought it?

Lopakhin: I bought it. (*Pause.* **Lyubov** *is overcome. Almost falls.* **Varya** *takes keys from her belt, throws them on floor in middle of room.*) I bought it—I need a drink—give me a second. I need a second to . . . (*Pause.*) Alright. We got to the auction. Deriganov was already there. Leonid Andreevich had only fifteen thousand. First this Deriganov bid *thirty*. Alright. That's how it is, I bid *forty*. He bids forty-five. I go to fifty, and by fives, alright, he goes by fives. I go by *tens*. Eighty? No I go *ninety* . . . *ninety*. The man says it is against you, sir—and then: I won! I *won*, I *did* it, and it's mine—the cherry orchard is *mine*. The cherry orchard is mine—I'm dreaming. It's alright. I'm living in a dream. I'm *drunk*. I just *imagined* it. Oh *God*. Could my father and my grandfather arise from their graves and look down: *Yermolai:* your *stupid, beaten, illiterate* . . . went barefoot in the winter . . . *Yermolai bought that estate.* The most beautiful . . . bought the estate *where you were slaves*. Where you could not come in the *kitchen*. *Yes. I'm* dreaming . . . a *fever* or . . . *these* things can't be real. (*Picks up keys, gentle smile. Orchestra is heard tuning up.*) Musicians. *Play. I* want to hear you play. *Watch* me—and *tell* how Yermolai Lopakhin took an ax, struck *down* . . . the cherry orchard. Watched the trees fall—to build *cottages*—so our grandchildren could have a new life—*MUSIC! (The music is playing.* **Lyubov** *has sunk into chair.*) Why didn't you listen to me? Why can't we go *past* this? Why do we have to cry?

Pishchik: Leave her alone. She's weeping. Let her weep. Come . . . let's . . .

Lopakhin: No! Not at all. *I* don't desire it—I want *music*. Here's the new *landlord*. Here he comes—the owner of the cherry orchard— (*He bumps into table. Almost knocks over candelabra.*) It's alright—I can pay for it.

Lopakhin *and* **Pishchik** *exit. Nobody left but* **Lyubov,** *sitting, crying. Music plays softly.* **Anya** *and* **Trofimov** *enter.* **Anya** *goes to* **Mama, Trofimov** *by door.*

Anya: Mama. My beautiful one. I love you. The cherry orchard is sold. It is no more. But you have your good, pure spirit—come—we'll go away from here—we'll plant a *new* orchard. A *better* orchard than this. And joy will settle on your spirit. Deep joy. Quiet joy. Like the sun at evening. Mama . . . (*Pause.*) Mama . . .

Act Four

A hum of voices is heard offstage.

Gaev (*off*): Thank you my friends—

Yasha: Simple folk. Good folk. Came to say "good-bye." Good simple folk. What do they understand?

The hum subsides. Enter **Gaev** *and* **Lyubov.** *She is pale.*

Gaev: Why did you do that, Lyuva?

Lyubov: I couldn't help it.

Gaev: To give them your *purse?*

Lyubov: I couldn't . . . (*Exit.*)

Lopakhin: Yes. Before we, just before we go—drink with me. One drink before parting . . . one glass. I should have brought a cold bottle from town—I found one at the station. Only one, but . . . *well.* Let's *drink*

it! No? Yes? . . . No? Ladies and Gentlemen . . .!!!
(*Pause.*) No? Alright—if I knew I wouldn't have
bought it . . . fine. I won't drink either. *Yasha, Yasha.*
Hey, my friend . . . come on. . . !

Yasha: One glass. To those who are departing. Good
luck and good— (*Drinks.*) This champagne's counterfeit—that's not the label—I assure you.

Lopakhin: Charged me ten rubles—oh *God* it's cold
here . . .

Yasha: No heat today. Why start up the fire—we're
leaving, anyway . . . *ha!*

Lopakhin: What are you laughing at?

Yasha: "Aha."

Lopakhin: October outside . . . sunny as summer.
Quiet. Good time to build. Good time to build for
oneself— (*Checks watch.*) My friends—let's try to . . .
(*pause*) let us try to remember: forty-six minutes to
train time—which means we have to leave in twenty
minutes—so let's get *about* it.

Trofimov (*enters*): I feel, it feels like we're leaving
right now. They brought the *horses* up . . . and where
are my galoshes? *I* can't find them. *Anya*—I . . . I
don't know where my galoshes are.

Lopakhin: I'm going to go down with you on the train.
I'm going to Kharkov. I'm going to spend the winter

there. (*Sighs.*) I can't stay around *here*—always hanging around, and talking. Talking . . . no *work* and you go mad. Pretty quickly, I think. That's what *I* do . . . I don't know. My hands feel like they belong to someone else.

Trofimov: Well, we're leaving and you can once again resume your rightful labor.

Lopakhin: Come on, have a drink.

Trofimov: No thank you.

Lopakhin: Alright. (*Pause.*) And you are off to. . . ? *Moscow.*

Trofimov: Yes. I'll go with them to town, and tomorrow to Moscow.

Lopakhin: Moscow. And put some life back in the old university. Eh? "Here he is again," the teachers'll say: "Now we can get back to some *real* learning!"

Trofimov: Why don't you shut up?

Lopakhin: How many years have you been down there?

Trofimov: Come up with a newer one, will you? You know, we're *leaving*, and we will not meet again— and, if I may, I'd like to leave you with a piece of advice: Don't make such grand gestures—I am speaking of your arms, your habit of waving them to make a point and I am also speaking of your gesture of the cottages—tear it down, build it up, own it, *destroy* it . . . (*Pause.*) Well—(*Pause.*) All the same . . . all the same, I have to admit some affection for you—you have good hands and you have a good soul.

Lopakhin (*embraces him*): My friend. *Farewell*—thank you. Thank you for everything—farewell—here . . . (*Reaches in his pocket.*)

Trofimov: What?

Lopakhin: I want you to have this.

Trofimov: What? What for?

Lopakhin: For the trip—

Trofimov: I don't need it—

Lopakhin: But you don't *have* any.

Trofimov: Yes. Thank you. I do. I've just got paid for a translation. I have it right . . . (*Pats pocket.*) But I do *not* have my galoshes.

Varya: Here—*relieve* me, I beg you. (*Throws him galoshes.*)

Trofimov: Varya the . . . these aren't mine. Why are you angry at me . . . Varya. *Varya*. These aren't my galoshes.

Lopakhin: Last spring I planted three hundred acres of poppy. And I *cleared* forty-thousand rubles. When they *bloomed* you would say that the sight of them *alone* was worth the trouble. So I say this. Forty thousand. A windfall . . . I don't need it—and I offer you a loan—because I can. I'm a *peasant*, alright? And that's the way I am. And you snub me.

Trofimov: Your father was a peasant and mine was a pharmacist. So what did that prove? Quintessentially nothing. (**Lopakhin** *takes out billfold.*) No, thank you. I said no—offer me what you like, two hundred thousand—I don't *want* it. *Why?* I'm a free man. And what you value, what beggars value, what the rich value, has no hold on me. It is a heat mirage. And my strength comes from this: I do not need it, and I do not need to believe in its worth—humankind is rising. To a higher good. To happiness. The highest possible on earth—and I am rising with it. In the front ranks.

Lopakhin: And will you get there?

Trofimov: Yes. I will get there. Or I will show others the way.

Axes heard.

Lopakhin: Well. Goodbye my friend. It's time—we think each other fools. But life goes on—and takes no notice—when I *work hard* over a period of time then I'm at peace, and it seems I feel . . . I know why I'm here. But how many in *Russia* have any *idea* why they're here? You know they said that Leonid An-

dreevich took a job at the bank. Six thousand a year—
he won't stick with it, though, he's too lazy.

Anya: My mother asks: would you please ask them not
to cut down the trees until she has left—

Trofimov: . . . A reasonable request.

Lopakhin: Yes, absolutely. Forgive me. (*Exits.*)

Anya: They took Firs to the hospital?

Yasha: One would suppose that he went this morning.

Anya: *Don't* tell me "one would suppose." Did they
take him to the hospital? Semon Panteleich.

Yasha: I *told* you they did. Why ask me ten times?

Yepikhodov: Firs. Firs. Our venerable Firs. Of many
summers—I would say he's gone beyond repair—and
should go to his just reward—I can but envy him. (*In
exiting, steps on hatbox.*) What did I. . . ? I could
have told you that. I *knew* it . . .

Yasha: "Endless Misfortune."

Varya (*offstage, simultaneously with "misfortune"*):
They took Firs to the hospital?

Anya: Yes.

Varya: We should have sent a letter to the doctor with him—

Anya (*simultaneously with "with"*)**:** We'll send it *after* him. (*Exits.*)

Varya: Yasha, your mother has come and wants to say good-bye.

Yasha: They'd try the soul of a saint.

Dunyasha *has been busying herself with luggage. Now she goes to* **Yasha.**

Dunyasha: Yasha. Why . . . why. . . ? One *look*. (*Pause.*) Won't you look at me? Yasha? One time. Can you abandon me? *Yasha.* Are you abandoning me? (*Crying and throwing herself on his neck.*)

Yasha: Oh please. Please. What is the good of tears? In six days I'll be in Paris. Tomorrow. We will be on the express. And roll. Vive la France! And goodbye to this. Goodbye to ignorance—and "country charm"— and there's an end, alright? And now stop crying. And conduct yourself with dignity and have some self-respect.

Dunyasha: Write me from Paris, Yasha. I loved you. I loved you so—I am a tender being, Yasha . . .

Gaev: We should be going.

Yasha: Ah ah ah! They're coming—

Enter **Lyubov, Gaev, Anya,** *and* **Charlotta.**

Gaev: We should be going—no time left, most of it gone . . . who smells of herring?

Lyubov: Now. Let's all be seated—in the *carriages* in twenty *minutes,* ready to go: goodbye dear house— old grandfather winter will pass—spring will arrive— and you will be gone—and they will tear you down. How much these walls have seen. (*Kisses* **Anya.**) My radiant angel—my life—your eyes are like diamonds. Are you happy?

Anya: Yes.

Lyubov: *Very?* Tell me . . .

Anya: Yes. Very.

Lyubov: Yes?

Anya: A new life is beginning. Mama.

Gaev: And in fact, you know, it would seem that that's true. Before the orchard was sold we were anxious, *worried,* we decide the question, when we finally "*decided.*" It, and everything grew calm. Has its points of *cheer*—and look at me? An old "banker"—a "financier." Rail first, black three cushions, then the red—and you, Lyuba—you look much better, no— *unquestionably*—

Lyubov: Yes. My nerves are better—this is true. And I'm sleeping again. Yasha—take my things out—it's time. (*To* **Anya:**) My darling—we will see each other soon. In Paris I'll be living on the money your grandmother sent to buy the estate. It won't last long—

Anya: You'll come back soon. Mama. You will won't you? When I pass my tests at school I'll work. I'll help you. We'll work together—we'll . . . we'll read—on autumn evenings; *everything* . . . we'll . . . a whole *world* will open to us. *Mama.* (*Pause.*) Mama. Come back to us.

Lyubov: I will. My precious one.

Enter **Lopakhin** *and* **Charlotta** *singing.*

Gaev: Charlotta: *Toujours gai!*

Charlotta (*holding a baby swaddled in her arms*): My little one: farewell. (*Child cries.*) My heart weeps for you—but . . . (*She drops the bundle—it is only a towel.*) Can someone here find me a position here? I can't continue with these . . .

Lopakhin: We'll find you one, Charlotta Ivanovna, don't you worry.

Gaev (*simultaneously with "worry"*): Everyone's throwing us over. We've become redundant.

Charlotta: And where can I live? Nowhere to live in *town. . . !* (*Sighs.*) Oh well— (*Sings.*)

Lopakhin: And behold!

Pishchik *enters.*

Pishchik: Oh my God let me catch my breath . . . oh
. . . most esteemed friends . . . oh—could I have a
glass of water?

Gaev: Come to beg for money . . . *sinner*—go and sin
no more. (*Exits.*)

Pishchik: I haven't had the pleasure of being here so
long . . . I . . . you . . . (*To* **Lopakhin:**) I'm glad to see
you . . . a *great* man . . . take . . . (*Presses money on
him.*) Here is, here . . . four hundred rubles . . . I
have eight hundred and forty left—

Lopakhin: Just like a dream. Alright. Where did you
get it. . . ?

Pishchik: I . . . one moment . . . *oh* it's hot here . . .
you won't . . . listen to . . . they came to my place—
Englishmen. Alright. They find some white "clay" in
the ground— (*To* **Lyubov:**) And to you my *most* fair,
most kind . . . (*Gives money.*) And the rest to fol-
low . . . (*Drinks water.*) Just now—a man on the
railroad was telling me some great philosopher ad-
vises jumping off of roofs—well well, he says *"jump"*
and the, the whole problem . . . (*Of glass.*) Could I
have some more?

Lopakhin: The Englishmen . . .

Pishchik: I signed over the *land* to them, small plot, twenty-four years, now, now, excuse me but I must press on—*Znoikov,* to *Kardamonov* . . . I'm . . . I owe *everybody*—Wednesday, I'll be back to . . .

Lyubov: We're leaving for town. And tomorrow I go abroad.

Pishchik: Excuse. . . ? (*Pause.*) To town? (*Pause.*) To. . . ? Oh . . . oh well . . . you know, I'm going to look at furniture . . . I'll miss you . . . Nothing. It's a parting—be happy and God will help you. Everything in this world has an end. And when you hear *I* have come to my end—*remember* this *horse* that I am, and say: "Once in the world there lived a man, etcetera, Simeonov-Pishchik, who did this and that and now God rest his soul." (*Pause.*) What weather. (*Pause.*) I . . . well. Alright—oh . . . (*Goes off. Comes back.*) Dashenka said to send her best . . . (*Exits.*)

Lyubov: And now I suppose we can go. Two, I have two things, *Firs,* is he? He's *ill* . . . we have five minutes, we can . . .

Anya: No, Mama—he's in the hospital. Yasha sent him this morning.

Lyubov (*simultaneously with "morning"*): Then: second is Varya. She's used to getting up early and working late. Now she has nothing to do she's like a fish out of water. She's grown *thin,* she *weeps* . . . you know, Yermolay Alexeevich, I dreamed of *giving* her to you . . . and it's seemed for so long you would be married . . . (*Whispers to* **Anya,** *who beckons to* **Charlotta.** *They exit. To* **Lopakhin:**) Now: she loves you; and I see that she suits your fancy too, is this not. . . ? And I say why *is* it that you, two . . . that you don't get together and I do not understand.

Lopakhin: I do not understand myself. And I admit it's strange. So strange. I . . . There's nothing for it. Let's *do* it. Now, right now, while there's still—let's *finish* it . . . as I feel . . . I don't . . . I feel when you've *left* I couldn't *do* it.

Lyubov: *Excellent.* I'm . . . yes. I'm going to call her. *Varya!* Come here—*Varya!* Right now leave what you're doing and come here.

Takes **Yasha. Yasha** *exits with her.*

Lopakhin (*sighs; softly*): Yes. Yes. Yes. (*Looks at watch.*)

Pause. Behind door, smothered laughter, whispering and then **Varya** *enters.*

Varya: That's odd. I can't find it anywhere.

Lopakhin: What are you looking for?

Varya: I know I *packed* it, and, uh . . . (*Pause.*)

Lopakhin: And. And where are *you* off to, Varvara Mikhailovna?

Varya: Where am I off to? To the Rogulins—I've agreed with them that I'd do their housekeeping.

Lopakhin: The Rogulins. In Yashnevo. What is that? About seventy kilometers . . .

Varya: Mm.

Lopakhin: So. (*Pause.*) And so the life has ended. In this house . . .

Varya: . . . Could I have packed it in the *trunk*. . . ? Yes. Life has ended. We . . .

Lopakhin: You know I'm going to Kharkov. On the train. I, uh, I'm leaving Yepikhodov here. I *hired* him . . .

Varya: You did . . .

Lopakhin: Yes, I . . . (*Pause.*) Last year. By this time. We'd already had snow. But now it's . . . it's quite. (*Pause.*) Sunny . . . *cold* . . . it's . . . three degrees of frost . . .

Varya: Yes? I haven't looked. Our thermometer's broken. (*Pause. He starts to move toward her.*)

Voices Offstage.

Voice Offstage: Yermolay Alexeevich.

Lopakhin: *Yes! Eh,* yes . . . *I'm* coming. . . !

Anton Chekhov

He exits. **Varya** *sitting on floor. Cries, puts head in bundle of clothes.*

Lyubov (*enters*): What happened? (*Pause.*) We have to go.

Varya: Yes. It's time Mamentchka. (*Sighs.*) Well, I'll be at the Rogulins today, if I can make the train . . .

Lyubov: *Anya. Let's go.*

Anya: We're going.

Enter **Anya, Gaev, Charlotta.** *Servants and drivers gather.* **Yepikhodov** *busies himself with luggage.*

Lyubov: Alright. Now. That's it. We must go.

Anya: We're going.

Gaev: My friends. My . . . dear, dear kind friends— abandoning this house forever. Can I hold my tongue? Can I keep silent? Can I . . . *stifle* those feelings which even now, suffuse . . .

Anya: *Uncle.*

Varya: Uncle. It's not . . . it's not . . .

Gaev (*pause*): Got four, going for five. Kiss off the *white* . . . rebound . . . (*Pause.*) I am silent.

Enter **Trofimov** *and* **Lopakhin.**

Trofimov: *Hmmm!* Ladies and gentlemen. It's time to go.

Lyubov: I must sit here. One moment. It is as if I never saw this house. What kind of *walls*. What *ceilings* . . . I must stare at them with greed. With such love . . .

Gaev: When I was six years old. I remember. Trinity Day. I sat in the window and watched father walking off to church.

Lyubov: V'they got the luggage in?

Lopakhin: It seems. Yes. (*To* **Yepikhodov.**) You'll see that everything's taken care of.

Yepikhodov (*hoarsely*)**:** Rest your mind about that, Yermolay Alexeevich.

Lopakhin (*simultaneously with "Alexeevich"*)**:** What's the matter with your voice?

Yepikhodov: I . . . I was drinking water and it went down the wrong way.

Yasha: Bravissimo.

Lyubov: We will leave and no one will remain.

Lopakhin: Not until spring. (**Varya** *pulls out umbrella as if she were going to hit someone.* **Lopakhin** *pretends to be frightened.*) What are you. . . ?

Varya: *Ah,* I . . . (*Pause.*)

Trofimov: Well *gentlefolk.* Let us assume our places in the carriages—it's time, the train . . .

Varya: Petya! I see your galoshes! How can you wear such *old* and *dirty* . . .

Trofimov (*putting on galoshes*): Ladies and gentlemen, let us go.

Gaev: Train. Station. Reverse to the rail . . . one cushion . . .

Lyubov: Let's go.

Anya: Farewell house—farewell. Goodbye, old life.

Trofimov: Hail to the *new* life.

Trofimov *exits with* **Anya. Varya** *looks around room and exits.* **Yasha** *and* **Charlotta** *with dog go out.*

Lopakhin: *Well* then. (*Pause.*) 'Til *spring. Out.* And we *leave*—my *friends.* Until we meet again—

He exits. **Lyubov** *and* **Gaev** *remain. They throw themselves on one another's necks crying.*

Gaev: Sister. Sister . . . oh, my sister . . .

Lyubov: My dear precious beautiful orchard . . . my life. My youth. My happiness. Goodbye.

Anya (*offstage*): Mama!

Offstage. **Trofimov** *blows whistle.*

Lyubov: I look upon these walls for the last time . . . in the room where my sainted mother walked . . .

Gaev: . . . Sister mine—sister mine.

Anya (*offstage*): *Mama!*

Trofimov (*offstage*): Let's go! Let's go.

Lyubov (*simultaneously with* "go"): We are coming . . .

Trofimov blows whistle. They exit. Heard keys locking doors, then carriages driving off. Quiet. Ax on trees heard. Enter **Firs**.

Firs (*at door*): *That's* locked. (*Pause.*) They've all gone. They've all gone and forgotten me. Alright. And I'll *bet* he did not put on his overcoat. (*Pause.*) Oh yes. Yes. (*Pause.*) Oh yes. You can't watch them all the time. (*Pause.*) Life has passed. I did not even live. Nothing left. No strength. No help for it, I'll just lie here for a little . . . (*Pause.*) You old fool . . .